STORY: JEREMY WHITLEY • ART: EMILY MARTIN
COLORS: KELLY LAWRENCE • LETTERS: DAVE DWONCH

Bryan Seaton - Publisher • Kevin Freeman - President • Dave Dwonch - Creative Director • Shawn Gabborin - Editor In Chief
Jamal Igle - Director of Marketing • Social Media Director - Jim Dietz • Chad Cicconi - Princess in Waiting • Colleen Boyd - Associate Editor

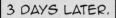

GENTLEMEN...

...MY WIFE AND I HAVE BEEN HAVING SOME RATHER VEXING PROBLEMS. HER WORRIES ARE SO GREAT SHE HAS TAKEN ABED ALL THIS LAST WEEK.

WHAT A FEEBLE CREATURE *WOMAN* IS.

I HAVE DONE A GREAT DEAL OF THINKING ON HOW TO BEST FIX THESE PROBLEMS. I HAVE DRAWN BUT ONE CONCLUSION.

THAT IS WHY I HAVE SUMMONED YOU, THE GREATEST KNIGHTS IN ALL THE LAND.

SIR ROCKS THE MIGHTY, A MAN REPORTED TO HAVE BESTED A TROLL IN BOTH AN EATING COMPETITION AND A WRESTLING MATCH... SIMULTANEOUSLY.
YOU THINK TROLLS ARE NASTY, YOU SHOULDA SEEN MY MA!
SIR GAHIJI THE HUNTER, WHO IS SAID TO HAVE SLAIN A GIANT ELE-PHANT WITH ONLY A PAIR OF BRASS KNUCKLES.
ELEPHANTS ALWAYS LEAD WITH THE JAB.
SIR RAPHAEL THE HANDSOME, RUMORED TO HAVE SEDUCED AND KILLED A SIREN, BOTH WITH THE SAME ROSE.
IT IS A SAD TRUTH THAT EVERY ROSE HAS ITS THORN.
OOOH, I SHOULD WRITE THAT DOWN.

SIR WALSH THE BRAGGART, A MAN WHOSE ESCAPES ARE NEARLY AS LEGENDARY AS THE INDECENT ACTS THAT NECESSITATE THEM..

THE HEART WANTS WHAT THE HEART WANTS.

IS IT MY FAULT THAT MINE WANTED TO STUFF A COOKED TURKEY ON THE DUCHESS' HEAD?

SIR ZACHARY THE PURE, A MAN SO PURE OF THOUGHT AND INTENTION THAT HE HAS TAMED WILD BEASTS WITH A TOUCH OF HIS HAND.

ALL CREATURES INNATELY DESIRE TO SERVE THE GODS.

SIMPLY NOT ALL OF THEM KNOW IT YET.

AND MY FIERCEST OF FRIENDS, A MAN WHO NONE HAVE SEEN IN YEARS, BUT WHOSE TALES ARE TOLD BY GORGONS TO SCARE THEIR CHILDREN.

THE BLACK KNIGHT.

...

NOW, I HAVE HAD A DWARVEN SMITH MAKE SOME VERY SPECIAL WEAPONS FOR EACH OF YOU, SPECIFICALLY DESIGNED FOR DRAGON SLAYING.

YOU CAN PICK THEM UP ON YOUR WAY OUT.

HA! YOU'RE A FOOL WALSH!

I'LL TELL YOU RIGHT NOW, I'LL HAVE ANGELICA.

WHAT GOOD'S HAVING A WOMAN IF EVERY OTHER MAN ISN'T JEALOUS OF ME FOR HAVING HER?

THE YOUNG ONES ARE FINE TO LOOK AT BUT I'LL TAKE ALIZE. AS THE OLDEST, SHE'S ALREADY GOT THE TRAINING TO COOK A GOOD MEAL. YOU CAN STARVE WITH YOUR MUSE.

YOU BRUTES ARE FAR TOO SUPERFICIAL. I LONG FOR THE SAD ROMANCE THAT HAUNTS ANGOISSE'S SOFT FOOT- STEPS.

I WOULD ASK FOR ANDREA OR ANTONIA, THOUGH I HEAR THEY ARE INSEPARABLE.

YOU ALL SEEK TREASURES THAT ARE ALREADY SPOILED. WHAT GOOD IS A WIFE IF SHE IS TOO OLD TO BE TRAINED?

I WOULD HAVE APPALONIA AND MAKE HER THE WIFE I NEED WHEN SHE COMES OF AGE.

SO... WHERE ARE YOU HEADED?

TO SEE THE MOST BEAUTIFUL WOMAN IN ALL THE LAND!

THE WOMAN WHO INSPIRED EVERY POEM I'VE EVER WRITTEN.

MY MUSE!

SHE IS THE SUN, THE MOON, AND THE STARS. HER SKIN IS THE COLOR OF THE ALDER TREE AND HER EYES GLEAM LIKE STARS IN THE DARK NIGHT.

HER BODY IS THE SHAPE THE GODS MEANT WHEN THEY SPOKE THE WORD WOMAN. HER HANDS ARE SOFT AND PETITE, BUT CAN MOVE MEN WITH A MERE BRUSH.

WOW, YOU'VE REALLY GOT A THING FOR THIS GIRL, HUH?

A... *THING?* TO CALL A LOVE LIKE THIS A *THING* IS TO BEFOUL AND DEBASE THE NAME OF *LOVE.*

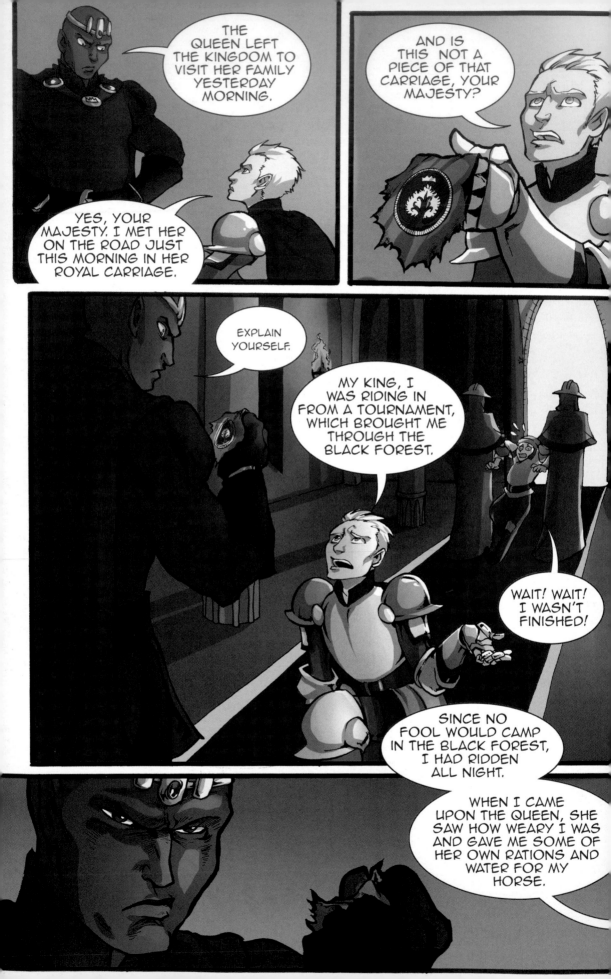

"WE KEPT COMPANY FOR A FEW MOMENTS BEFORE SHE CONTINUED EASTWARD WHILE I ATE AND WATERED MY HORSE.

IN A FLASH, ANOTHER KNIGHT PASSED.

I SWEAR IT WAS THE BLACK KNIGHT.

ON HIS HORSE'S BACK WAS A LARGE BUNDLE AND I SWEAR ONE OF HER GLOVES HUNG FROM IT.

I DID NOT KNOW WHAT COULD MAKE THE BLACK KNIGHT RIDE SO QUICKLY, BUT I FEARED FOR THE QUEEN.

WHAT I FOUND THERE WAS WORSE THAN I COULD HAVE IMAGINED.

THE SIDES OF THE CARRIAGE WERE SHREDDED AS IF BY GREAT CLAWS AND THE WHOLE BODY OF IT CRACKED AND POPPED WITH FLAMES.

ALL THAT WAS LEFT OF THE QUEEN WAS HER TRUNK, WHICH HAD BEEN EMPTIED AND ABANDONED. AND I WAS NOT THE ONLY ONE THERE."

MY KNIGHTS, TAKE MY HORSE AND GO BACK OUT OF THE FOREST ON THE PATH WE CAME ON.
DO NOT LEAVE THE PATH.
ND LEAVE YOU RE, SIRE? WHAT WILL YOU DO?
I HAVE SOME QUESTIONS THAT NEED ANSWERING FROM THE RESIDENTS OF THIS FOREST.
BE SURE TO STAY ON THE PATH. THERE ARE THINGS IN THIS FOREST MORE DANGEROUS THAN YOU KNOW.
BUT SIRE, WHAT OF THE ELVES? OR THE WOLVES?
THIS FOREST HAS ALREADY KILLED ME *ONCE*.
I'D LIKE TO SEE IT TRY AGAIN.

SWISSH!

SWOOF!

TELL ME SOMETHING. THAT DAY WHEN YOU CAME FOR THE BLACK KNIGHT AND I IN THE FOREST, HOW DID YOU KNOW TO COME?

WAS IT TO SAVE ME OR FIGHT THE ELVES?

IT WAS NEITHER.

YOUR COMPANION SOUGHT US OUT BEFOREHAND. ASKED FOR OUR HELP.

THE BLACK KNIGHT SPOKE TO YOU? I'VE NEVER HEARD HIM *SPEAK.*

PERHAPS YOU SHOULD LISTEN HARDER. YOU ALWAYS HEAR MORE WHEN YOU *DO.*

THAT FRIEND OF YOURS STAYED WITH YOU FOR A WEEK WHILE YOU HEALED.

THAT VOICE LED YOU OUT OF YOUR SICKNESS.

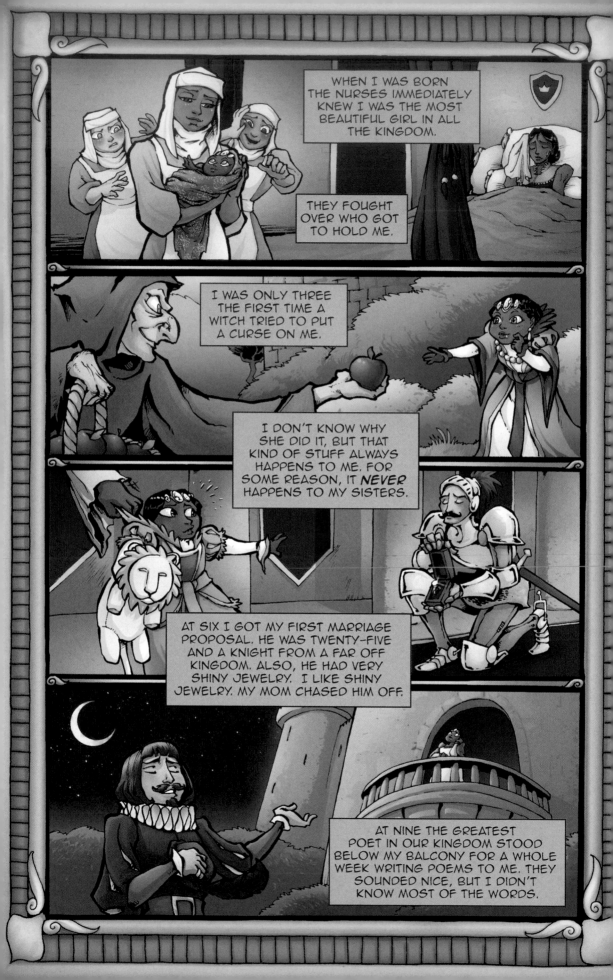

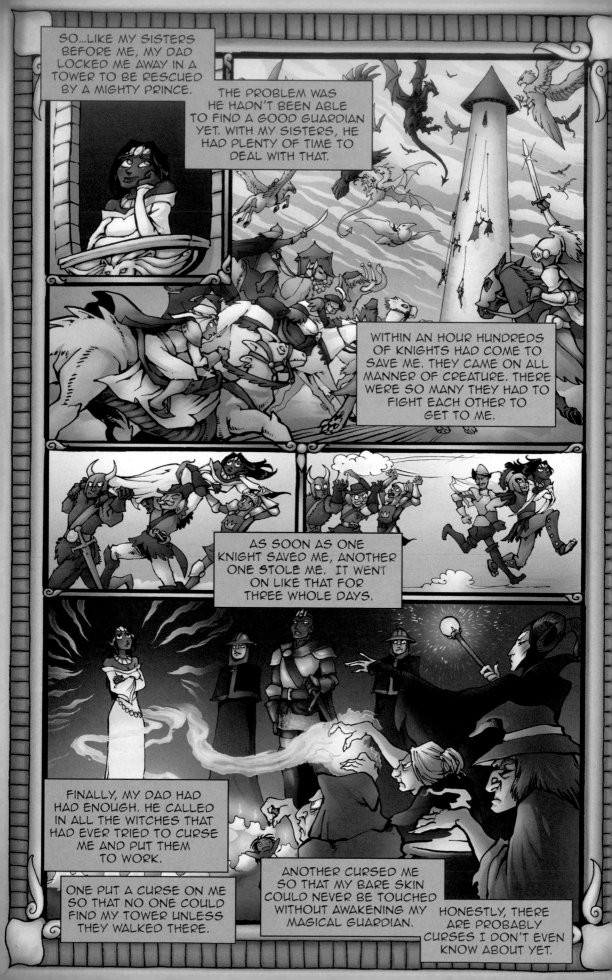

$3.99

$3.99

Girls Who Fight Boys

STORY: JEREMY WHITLEY
ART: EMILY C. MARTIN
COLORS: SOOJIN PAEK
LETTERS: DAVE DWONCH

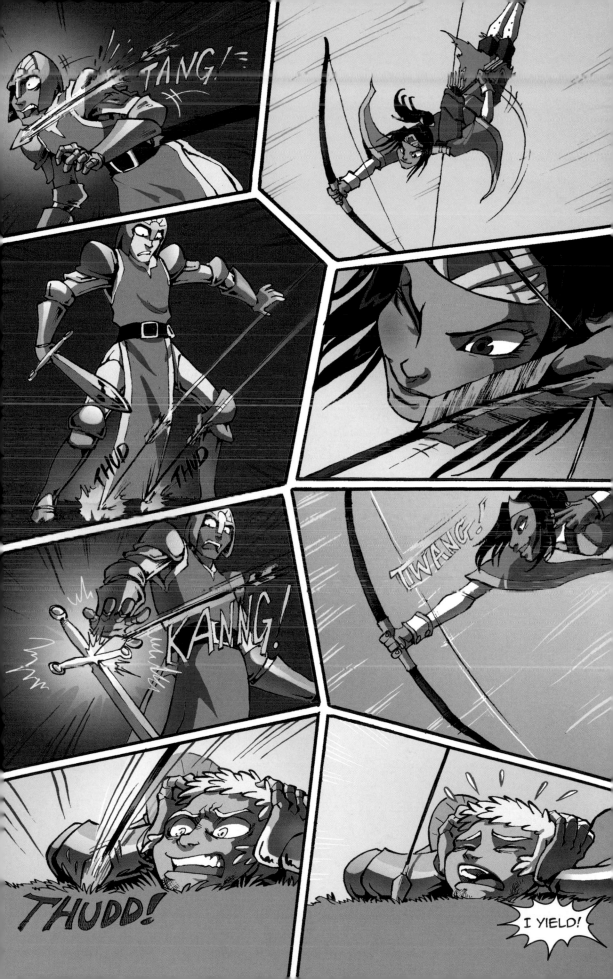